MINI SA

THE ADVENTURE STARTS HERE ...

SUFFOLK

First published in Great Britain in 2009 by
Young Writers, Remus House, Coltsfoot Drive,
Peterborough, PE2 9JX
Tel (01733) 890066 Fax (01733) 313524

SB ISBN 978-1-84924-146-5

FOREWORD

Since Young Writers was established in 1990, our aim has been to promote and encourage written creativity amongst children and young adults. By giving aspiring young authors the chance to be published, Young Writers effectively nurtures the creative talents of the next generation, allowing their confidence and writing ability to grow.

With our latest fun competition, *The Adventure Starts Here...*, primary school children nationwide were given the tricky challenge of writing a story with a beginning, middle and an end in just fifty words.

The diverse and imaginative range of entries made the selection process a difficult but enjoyable task with stories chosen on the basis of style, expression, flair and technical skill. A fascinating glimpse into the imaginations of the future, we hope you will agree that this entertaining collection is one that will amuse and inspire the whole family.

CONTENTS

Westley Middle School

THE MINI SAGAS

THE FAIRY WITH NO POWER

Once upon a time there was a fairy; she was sad and alone because she had no power. The Fairy Queen whispered, 'Don't worry, you will get your powers soon.'

A week later, the young fairy got her powers, she was so pleased she became a Rose Fairy.

SCARLET DAVENPORT (9)

Bacton Community Primary School

POP STAR HAMSTERS

It was dark and the hamsters were backstage,
suddenly the lights came on and the music started.
Then the hamsters walked on stage and started
playing their pencil guitar, rubber drums and singing
in their carrot microphones.
Then something went wrong, they started eating
their microphones.

POPPY SEAMAN (8)
Bacton Community Primary School

A TRIP TO THE ZOO

A little girl was at the zoo, she visited the dolphins.
They got her soaked. On her way home, a little dog
followed her. She took him home and looked after
him.
The zoo called and asked for their dog back, what
was she going to do?

ESME FEAVEARYEAR (8)
Bacton Community Primary School

STORE WARS

The trolleys were winning against the tills with their
squash lasers and lemon bombs. *Boom!*
Suddenly, the tills let some mini store ships loose!
The tills had laser readers that began cutting through
the trolleys!

OWEN GODDARD (8)
Bacton Community Primary School

THE ICE CREAM PALACE

One hot day, Sarah, with her six children, were sitting in an ice cream palace. Suddenly, the palace started falling down. Sarah and her six children were having the best day of their life. Then it started to drip really bad and fell down. The six children cried and cried.

LAUREN FIRMAN (9)
Bacton Community Primary School

THE FAIRY WHO LOST HER WINGS

Once upon a time, there was a fairy called the Scarlet Pimpernel. One shimmering morning, Scarlet woke up. She looked on her back, there were no glittery wings. Scarlet was worried. She thought, *maybe I just can't see them!*

She was the Scarlet Pimpernel fairy with no wings forever!

AMARA GUTTERIDGE (8)

Bacton Community Primary School

THE MAGIC CHRISTMAS

One cold, snowy Christmas morning I woke up and thought I had just heard the bells from Santa's reindeer. I looked out of the window and saw all the Christmas lights shining across the valley. I went down the stairs and saw all the presents waiting to be unwrapped.

JESSICA ARMSTRONG (8)
Bacton Community Primary School

THE MAGIC TABLET

Once there was a magic wizard who lived with his apprentice, Luke Skywalker. One day they went to a cave and found a magic tablet but it was in a forcefield. Luke broke it with his magic, took it and destroyed it because it led to a black hole.

MEGHAN ARNOLD (9)

Bacton Community Primary School

THE LITTLE SHOE

I woke up with a start. I went downstairs. After my breakfast, I went back upstairs. Suddenly ... I felt something under my foot. I picked my foot up, it was a tiny shoe. I couldn't believe my eyes. I went into my bedroom. I saw a fairy.

ELIZA SEAMAN (8)

Bacton Community Primary School

THE GREEDY GENIES

Once upon a time there were genies that could grant wishes. One bright, shimmering day, at the crack of dawn, the Emperor of a kingdom far away in India, paid a visit to the powerful genies' home. The genies were fed up so they had some fun with the wish!

FREYA PATERSON (8)
Bacton Community Primary School

THE CHRISTMAS SIMPSONS

Once upon a time, there was the Simpsons family. They were looking forward to Christmas. On Christmas Day they saw that there were loads of presents so they opened them happily and quietly. Then they saw there was one missing. They were very annoyed and disappointed.

HARRY SIMPSON (9)
Bacton Community Primary School

THE CRAZY DANCING XMAS TREE

Once upon a time I was lying in bed. I heard a rustle and it was my Christmas tree, so I went downstairs and you'll never guess what I saw. I saw my Christmas tree dancing. I was so surprised. Soon as I saw it, I burst out laughing …

MILLIE TURVEY (8)
Bacton Community Primary School

SUPER CAT

One stormy day, a cat got struck by lightning, it turned into Super Cat. On Monday Super Cat saved Robbie Williams from Old Hag Mag. On Tuesday he saved Loopy Lauren from the stinky toilet. On Wednesday he saved Jumpy Jessica from Evil Ella, but she suffocated him to death.

JESSICA RICE (8)
Bacton Community Primary School

THE THREE LITTLE PIGS

Once upon a time there were three little pigs. One day the pigs were naughty so Mum Pig decided that she would send them away. They all made their own houses.
One sunny day, the wolf came along and blew the houses down!

ELLA TOMLIN (8)
Bacton Community Primary School

CHILDREN IN NEED AT BARDWELL

On Children In Need, Mrs Dodsworth drew a Pudsey on the floor and we put coins round it. We also had a sale. We raised £117. The School Council did the stalls, it was very good and we wore pyjamas and crazy hats. We had a great day!

MATTHEW WHITELOCK (9)

Bardwell VC Primary School

DISASTER

What a nice day. It's so sunny. Err, what's happened?
It's like the sun's turned off! Something's going on …
but how could they not tell me? I know, I will go and
watch TV to pass the time. *Crash!* What's that? Oh
no! What am I going to do now?

JASMINE CLACKETT (9)

Bulmer St Andrew's CE Primary School

ATTACKING RABBIT

It was a dark, stormy night when all of a sudden,
an attacking rabbit jumped out the hedge and tried
to attack two people. They stopped him with their
special force ...
They took the rabbit to the vet and found out that he
had the brain of a devil!

KIERAN MARSHALL (10)

Bulmer St Andrew's CE Primary School

HO, HO, HO

In the dead of night, a person named Harry was walking in the woods. *What was that?* he thought. He heard sleigh bells and a clanging of 'Ho, ho, ho.' 'Yes they are definitely sleigh bells!' He went to investigate. Yes, there it was! He could not believe his eyes!

JACK EDWARDS (9)
Bulmer St Andrew's CE Primary School

THE MONSTER OF BIZZARO

We had just landed on the sandy beach at Bizzaro. We headed into the dense jungle, close to the beach. We soon arrived at a clearing in the jungle. I was sitting down having a drink, when suddenly a giant hairy hand grabbed me by the throat! Then nothing ...

ANNA ADAMS (10)
Bulmer St Andrew's CE Primary School

THE WAY BACK HOME

It was on the way back home. Our friend was with
us, but decided to go back through the forest. I heard
a scream, I am sure it was him.
I couldn't bear this for much longer … but it made
me think, *people who go in, never come out again!*

HARRIET PHILO POWELL (11)
Bulmer St Andrew's CE Primary School

THE NIGHT BEFORE CHRISTMAS

It was Christmas Eve. I suddenly woke up, there it was, a twinkling outside. Could it be? I slowly got up and peaked out the window. There, in the snow, stood the eight reindeer and Santa. A flash of light, I blinked and he was gone, in the frost.

NAOMI BISSET (10)
Bulmer St Andrew's CE Primary School

STUCK IN THE MUD!

James was out in the muddy fields, counting his pigs. He only counted nine pigs and he knew that he had ten. His best pig called Pepper was missing. He was worried.

Suddenly he heard an oink in the mud. It was Pepper covered in mud. James was so happy.

HANNAH CUSHNEY (10)

Bulmer St Andrew's CE Primary School

CHRISTMAS DAY

It was Christmas Day. It should've been one of the happiest days of my life, but it wasn't. I saw something, maybe a devil, but whatever it was, it was coming to get me! The phone rang. I was the only one in the house, I picked it up …

OPHELIA MATHER (9)
Bulmer St Andrew's CE Primary School

DESERT ISLAND

Rumours get passed on, secrets get passed on, but what you don't know is that truth gets passed on, and truth is one scary nightmare. It isn't a dream. You are here, you're at the desert island. This will be the last time you scream …

ZOË COYNE (10)
Bulmer St Andrew's CE Primary School

MYSTERIOUS RED FIGURE

Sweating like I had been swimming, I ran into the graveyard. I looked around, the snake-like figure had gone. Then it happened, a bony, heavy hand grabbed my shoulder. I heard a deadly scream and I woke up. My door was slowly opening.

CHARLOTTE ROBINSON-SMITH (10)
Bulmer St Andrew's CE Primary School

BOO

It was Hallowe'en … when I looked out the door and saw a pair of glowing eyes. I went to see what it was, something grabbed me from the dark, I was scared and did not know what to do. Then I saw my dad and screamed …

DANIEL PARRETT (10)
Bulmer St Andrew's CE Primary School

CHRISTMAS EVE

It was Christmas Eve and everyone was in bed.
The whole place looked like a new planet of white.
I walked downstairs to investigate. It was Santa!
Right in front of me! So many presents, all for me! I
couldn't believe it! Was it real? I don't know …

TOMMY SHUTTLEWOOD (9)
Bulmer St Andrew's CE Primary School

HOME LOST

I woke up one morning and realised I wasn't at home. I got up and looked around. I heard a scream. I was terrified. Then a tap on my shoulder. I turned around, in front of me stood a kidnapper.

ELLIE TOOGOOD (11)
Bulmer St Andrew's CE Primary School

WHO!

I climbed out of my bed and crept downstairs. I saw someone there. I checked that it was not my mum and dad because they were in bed. But the person had a black belt and a red dress! I thought that it was someone dressed up like Santa.

GEMMA WICKER (9)

Bulmer St Andrew's CE Primary School

MYSTERY

We heard mysterious noises. All of a sudden, *bang!* My friend was dead. I had to carry on. At long last, I found the golden book. But the ghosts had found me, stealing my last chance to be safe. I felt a pinch, finally back in my bed … or not!

JACK BERKELEY (10)
Bulmer St Andrew's CE Primary School

I WISH I COULD FLY LIKE YOU

'I wish I could fly like you,' Caterpillar said to Robin.
'Well maybe one day that wish will come true!'
One night, Caterpillar stayed asleep until summer came. When he woke up, he had changed. He had wings.
From that day onwards, Caterpillar was a sky-gliding butterfly!

VANESSA CHANCE (10)

Bulmer St Andrew's CE Primary School

A DARK DEATH

On a dark, stormy night, I heard something downstairs. I got out of bed to have a look. Then someone grabbed my body and I was taken away to a place that was dark and gloomy. I was tied to a tree and left to die.

GEORGINA ROONEY (10)
Bulmer St Andrew's CE Primary School

WHAT HAPPENED?

What was happening? Nobody seemed to be
enjoying Christmas, as if it wasn't happening! My
friends just looked speechless. I didn't understand, no
trees, no trimmings! I was so confused.
I woke at 6am sharp with a big, big fright. I realised it
was all a dream, a bad dream!

SOPHIE MOUNTFORD (9)
Bulmer St Andrew's CE Primary School

WRONG WORDS!

Cinderella, dressed in yella, locked all her boyfriends in the cellar! Wait, they're the wrong words! Cinderella, dressed in yella, went to the ball and won her fella! But they're still the wrong words! Here we go again, Cinderella dressed in … oh forget it! They'll always be the wrong words!

ELISE INNES (9)
Cedarwood Primary School

ANGEL

Once the world was invaded by smoke and Heaven did not like it. It was sad. Everyone was coughing. It was getting in eyes. One angel called Sarah, ran into her house and said, 'Mum! Heaven's been invaded by smoke.'

Her mum looked out and fainted in Sarah's arms!

LUCY WEBSTER (8)

Cedarwood Primary School

MOUNT EVEREST

One day, when I was three, my dad took me to Mount Everest. It took seven days. My dad had to carry me all the way to the top. When we were halfway there, my dad was exhausted. He put me down. I slipped straight into my mum's arms.

JOSHUA GEDNY (8)
Cedarwood Primary School

THE SHADOWS

In the shadows, a strange person stood as hard as iron. It gloomed at me. It was a mystery. I moved away but it was stopping me, its hands were red. It charged towards me, I was petrified. It fired a ball at me, it knocked me out then ... *bang!*

JACK SKINGSLEY (8)
Cedarwood Primary School

ALONE ... STILL!

20 years ago, she waited, the clock ticking. 'Anyone
there?' The door creaked, suddenly light came in, a
shadow in the doorway. A hand grabbed her.
'You're not alone now!'
Her handsome prince came, swept her off her feet.
No, it was just Dad, back from the shops!

ABIGAIL BATES (10)
Cedarwood Primary School

THE RAINDROP THAT NEVER STOPPED

Once upon a time there was a raindrop that never stopped. It was raining for forty days and forty nights. Everyone went out in boats. All the animals tried to get on-board the Ark.

'Only two of each kind,' said Noah.

The raindrop was so tired it stopped ...

CARA HAVELL (9)
Cedarwood Primary School

THE WEEK OF DOOM

The lady screamed as she let her baby float over
the long winding river. Slowly the baby awoke and
wondered where he was. Try as he might, nobody
could hear his cries through the long, shaky reeds.
The baby screamed.
After a long week the poor baby slowly drowned.

JENNA BURROWS (9)
Cedarwood Primary School

LASER FIGHT

Lasers all around me, flying onto my pads with Ross,
George and all the rest.
'Help me,' said Ross.
I fought my way to Ross ... He was not there and no
one else was either. I was all on my own!

DYLAN BARRETT (9)
Cedarwood Primary School

RED EYE

I stood in the draughty cave. I crept in closer and saw two red eyes staring at me. I looked for my night-vision goggles but found they'd been ripped apart by something. I sprinted and stumbled. A sudden screech filled my ear. The red eyes came, I was trapped!

HARRY BOSTOCK
Charsfield CE (VC) Primary School

THE KILLER

Footprints in the mud. He staggered past me, not knowing the footprints ended. He caught my eye. I was in front of him … in front of the killer. I scrambled up the rocks. He grabbed me. I slipped. I hit my head. Blood dripped to the ground.

KASSI WATSON (10)
Charsfield CE (VC) Primary School

LOCKED

She slowly turned the key, twisted the handle and opened the door. Suddenly, a huge brown St Bernard flashed out of the door. She was in shock. She tried to hide, the doors were tightly locked. The front door slammed. She rattled the door. It was locked. She was trapped!

CHARLOTTE BOSTOCK (9)
Charsfield CE (VC) Primary School

THE SHADOW

It was a dark night in the haunted house. Snakes and rats all over the floor. It was as dirty as a junkyard. I crept along the creaky wooden floor. The stormy wind rattled like a hurricane. Suddenly, as I was going upstairs, a long shadow came over me.

JOSEPH WESTERN (9)
Charsfield CE (VC) Primary School

TRAPPED

I fired my acid gun at the locked door. I clambered through, I could hear a faint buzzing noise. I crept forwards only to find another locked door. I reached for my acid gun but it was gone. I turned back but the door had swung shut. I was trapped!

OLIVER ANDERSON (10)
Charsfield CE (VC) Primary School

HAUNTED HOUSE

Annie shouted, 'Help!'
Her friend, Gracie, screamed, 'Argh!'
Her best friend, Amy shouted, 'Mum!'
They saw a monster; it was green and hairy and had sharp claws. Annie and Amy ran away but Gracie stood there. She explained to her friends that it was just a robot.

CHARLIE FERGUSON (9)
Charsfield CE (VC) Primary School

THE CAVE!

I was feeling adventurous. I tiptoed inside the gloomy cave. Suddenly, I heard something. Luckily it was just a stick that had snapped under my feet. A corner was looming up. I peered round. There was a dark figure waiting there. I ran …

KATE FLETCHER (9)

Charsfleld CE (VC) Primary School

THE WOODEN CHEST

She opened the wooden chest. There was a bright glow. She saw glittering necklaces, rings, bracelets but there was something else moving. She saw a small hairy leg, then another, then another. She screamed, she didn't know what the creature was or how deadly it was going to be …

LAURA BRIGHT (10)

Charsfield CE (VC) Primary School

HORROR

A boy scuttled home on his bike. When he got home,
he thought that no one was around.
It was midnight. He heard wolves howling. The door
creaked open …
'Happy Hallowe'en!' he heard someone shout.
He got on his bike and sped away as if a ghost was
after him!

NOEL MANN (9)
Charsfield CE (VC) Primary School

A SUDDEN NOISE

He was watching TV when a sudden crashing noise came from his mum's house across the road. He ran over there to see what had gone wrong. He arrived but nobody was inside. He heard a muttering noise coming from the kitchen but nobody was there. He heard it again ...

ALEX HAYWARD (10)
Charsfield CE (VC) Primary School

CREATURE

The waves as fast as a cheetah, and the wind howling like a wolf over a nearby island. On one rocky ledge there was a dark cave as black as night, but, it wasn't just a cave. It was a home, a home to a gigantic creature.

FREDERICK YULE (10)
Charsfield CE (VC) Primary School

THE CREATURE

On Hallowe'en I was on my way back from the pictures when I heard a noise. It sounded as fierce as a Minotaur. Something came charging through the trees. I ran as fast as I could. The creature was gaining on me.

MOLLY LEE (9)
Charsfield CE (VC) Primary School

A BAD MISTAKE ...

Owen opened the door. He and Jim stepped inside.
The door slammed behind them. Jim said to Owen,
'This is scary, why did you drag me along?'
'Would you come alone?' asked Owen.
They looked around the room. Jim opened another
door. That was his final mistake!

OSCAR SPIVEY GREEN (10)
Charsfield CE (VC) Primary School

THE BLACK SORROWS

They're coming. All the sorrows are coming like they're going to take over the world. Every second the menacing figures are getting closer. The dark gloomy sky and a world full of shadows. Soon the world will be full of sorrows and sadness.

BOBBY FORD (10)

Charsfield CE (VC) Primary School

ROUND THE CASTLE WALLS

The huge black bear slammed the ground as it chased the diminutive hare. Round the castle doors, the bear came face to face with the lion, his rival. Unseen, the hare slipped away and the lion's roar ricocheted around the walls … Which of them would die?

PETER GUGENHEIM (10)

Charsfield CE (VC) Primary School

SHADOWS

As my feet crunched on the soft snow a whisper echoed in my ear. I turned to see the fast movement of a shadow and stood still wondering who it was. I screamed. Out from the bush came a face, it was kind and I saw my sister, Alex.

SHANNON FINBOW (12)
Combs Middle School

FOOTSTEPS

I walked faster, trying to get home to bed. *Crunch! Crunch!* I heard footsteps behind me. They got faster and faster. I turned around. Nothing. I carried on walking and I heard them again. I turned around again. Still nothing. I turned back and my parents were there in front!

JESSICA MOWLES (11)
Combs Middle School

WHO?

Clip-clop, clip-clop. I hurried on as the sound came closer and louder. I walked on quicker but still the sound came closer. As I walked up the road to my house, the person shouted, 'Hey!' It sounded familiar, but I wouldn't risk it, I ran.

'Wait!' shouted Dad.

KIRA RODEN (12)

Combs Middle School

DARKNESS

The moon hung low over the great African plain - illuminating the skeletal branches of the trees that stretched across the desolate landscape. Crouching under one was a dark deformed shape, and, as the moon reached its highest point in the sky, the light penetrated the shadows to reveal the lion.

MEGAN WILLIAMS (12)
Combs Middle School

NOTHING'S FAIR IN LOVE OR WAR!

Tom looked deeply into Anna's eyes. She could tell that she was not going to like what he was about to say.

'Well, we have been going out for seven days so I think I should move on.'

With that Tom turned and left. The tears would soon come. Soon.

WILLIAM SCOTT (12)

Combs Middle School

UNLUCKY

Dawn was casting spun gold threads across a rosy sky over Masai Mara game reserve. I leapt from my bed since there was a strange noise. I looked, a grand lion was infesting my room. That was the end of me. The twelfth of the twelfth, two thousand and twelve.

CHARLOTTE COLES-MORRIS (11)

Combs Middle School

THE GUN

'Hey!' the elderly man yelled after me. 'Get back here!'
I ran as fast as a cheetah, knocking a lady and her miniature dog aside. The man's voice faded gradually as I neared my house. I saw my house in the distance and ran towards it - pulling out a gun.

AMY QUIGLEY (12)

Combs Middle School

LOONY VILLAGERS

Dipstick Dana was Loonyville's greatest superhero. When she heard a piercing scream, she ran to the rescue. She knocked out Hannah Banana when she arrived. Unfortunately, Hannah Banana was the one screaming, so Dipstick Dana had to race to capture Corny Catherine. As usual Dipstick Dana was triumphant. Hooray!

LOUISE CLARKE (12)
Combs Middle School

CRASH

My heart was thumping hard against my chest. The two cars were about to collide with each other. Time went very slowly. I was waiting, waiting for the moment. *Crash!* Suddenly there was silence, then the scream of fire engines, flashing lights of police cars! Luckily nobody was hurt.

HANNAH-MAE COBBOLD (12)

Combs Middle School

SOMETHING

She walked into the isolated house. She jumped back, crushing something under her feet. She decided to walk on but as she did, she wished she hadn't. She turned around. Standing there was a massive thing looming over her, getting ready to pause and then attack …

EMILY WEBB (11)
Combs Middle School

TAKE TWO

We had just done the first take. It went terribly, the background came down. I had to put it up. It was high. As I climbed up, the wire on my belt got stuck, I was hanging by my fingers. What would happen to me?

'Take two,' said the director!

HOPE GUNN (12)
Combs Middle School

THE END

Jake and Leo were driving their camper van along the abandoned dusty road. They came across a stone. It had a small red dot on it. The camper van beeped. Jake and Leo jumped out of the car and sprinted as fast as they could. *Boom!* Was this the end?

REUBEN KNOCK (12)
Combs Middle School

MOONLIGHT

The moon was full and gave a peaceful glow to the gentle lake. Beth gazed happily out into the water. 'Hello! Beth?' a voice called out, breaking the silence. Beth gasped and ran, stumbling against the rotten root from the oak tree. Silently cursing the moonlight, she hid in shadows.

ALEXIS CURRIN (11)
Combs Middle School

THE CREATURE

There it was, standing in the dimly lit corridor. A dark, shadowy creature. It shrieked when I turned the bright lights on. It quickly covered its face as I walked past it with my cross necklace.
'Keep it away!' shrieked Dad.
'Oh it's just you!' I quickly replied. Strange!

HARRY MIDDLETON (11)
Combs Middle School

SILENT

The shadowy figure crept forward. Bright lights shone from the building illuminating more dark shapes. Further and further … closer, ever closer - not far. The gnarled trees cast a shadow over the field. He ran. The dark shapes chased him. He stumbled and fell …
'It!' shouted Dan as he grabbed Tom.

ETHAN POWELL (11)
Combs Middle School

THE PRETENDER

No one knows who he is. He has no fixed personality. He is a criminal mastermind. He breaks the law for fun. As he walks down the street, passing people, unaware of him, stop to say hello, he just walks on. He wants no friends. Because he is a pretender …

HARRY HOGG (11)
Combs Middle School

THAT NIGHT

One day I was walking down the street when all of a sudden I heard a whisper.
'See you soon,' a ghostly figure was whispering to me.
Later on, in the middle of the night, a deranged man with an axe, was cutting up a dead man.
'Argh!' I ran.

MARK ALLEN (12)
Combs Middle School

THING

I woke up and there it was. I had to stop it or
someone was going to get hurt. I turned and hit it.
Screaming, screeching, it died.
I never found out what it was. I just call it … Thing.

YASMIN ARCHER (11)
Combs Middle School

IMAGINATION

I crossed the slippery road, there was a dark figure in the distance. A dark figure following me. I quickened my walk until I was standing outside my house. I ran in, constantly checking over my shoulder. I kept telling myself that there was nobody there - it was my imagination.

PAIGE QUIGLEY (12)
Combs Middle School

WATER

A cry. 'The wall's breached.' The water gushed in. I watched it all through a live video link. I felt like a coward, sitting in my watertight room. At least I did, until the door started creaking under pressure. I should have felt safe. But the heart-stopping screams didn't.

CALLUM RENTON (11)
Combs Middle School

DAY 1

On Thursday, I had a very creepy dream - that every person in the entire world had disappeared! I was frightened and very confused. Feeling like I should scream, I ran into my bedroom. I was shaken, as I knew that this was my worst nightmare!

HOLLY PARRY (11)
Combs Middle School

THE FINGER!

He slowly walked into the darkened room and looked around. As he shouted out hello something rattled outside on the window. Quickly turning his head to face the window, he saw a bony finger point towards the bookcase. He moved the book aside and read the message.
'Start running, fast!'

SHANNON THURGOOD (11)
Combs Middle School

FIRST SNOW

Anna was walking home. It felt especially cold to her because only a month ago, she had moved from Jamaica to England. She arrived home and warmed up by the fire. She looked out of the window and snowflakes were falling!

'This is what snow's like, it's beautiful!' she gasped.

ZOE PARSONS (12)

Horringer Court Middle School

IT

I arrived home and it was mysteriously quiet. As I heard a cackling shriek from upstairs, I slowly tiptoed up. I froze. Blue sparks were shooting out from under the door. I heard a scream then, without thinking, I screamed, 'Stop!' and burst through the door. Then I saw it …

LEWIS HOWELL (9)
Horringer Court Middle School

SUPERCAT

Supercat could fly and lift cars with one paw. A scary
shark was thrashing and gnashing at everything on
the beach. Supercat growled, 'That brute is spoiling
everybody's fun!'
He flew down and threw the shark far out to sea.
Everybody cheered, 'Thanks Supercat!'
Supercat sped off.
'That was purr-fect!'

WILLIAM COOKE WHARTON (9)

Horringer Court Middle School

A CHRISTMAS DREAM

As I came closer to the snow-covered building, I
came closer to my dream. I was going to meet him,
I was actually going to meet him. I was ecstatic. My
hands were trembling as I got closer and closer. Then
I was with Father Christmas.
Happy Christmas everyone!

SOPHIE PARSONS (10)
Horringer Court Middle School

GOAT TRAIL

Last summer, I went to the zoo to visit the goats and the gate was left open so they followed me out. Luckily I had sandwiches and on the way, I left a trail of breadcrumbs to the goats' area. The goats ate the crumbs and were back, safe.

AMELIA PETTITT (9)
Horringer Court Middle School

THE DEAL

'Where is the money, Jones?'
'I don't have all the money yet, I just need a little more time.'
'I warned you! Consider your family deleted forever!' shouted Alex.
'No,' yelled Jones.
'Take care of him, Goons.'
From that day no one saw Jones or his family ever again.

SAM FARRANT (10)
Horringer Court Middle School

STAR WARS WITH DOBBY

On the planet Naboo, Dobby was in a close encounter with Darth Vader. Dobby burped and Darth Vader fainted. Dobby said, 'Bad Dobby! Bad, bad, bad Dobby!' He killed himself.
In Heaven, he said, 'Bad Dobby!' He stepped on God's foot and shouted, 'Bad Dobby.' Then went to Hell.

CHARLIE CLAYTON (10)
Horringer Court Middle School

GUNSHOT

Joe was walking along a dark alleyway in London.
Joe was clutching a knife. Suddenly a masked man
jumped out in front of Joe, he reacted at once
and pulled out the knife. The man had a gun and
threatened, 'Money now!'
Joe refused. *Bang!* Joe was shot.

MICHAEL FARRANT (10)
Horringer Court Middle School

NO HIDING PLACE

Police sirens start to roar. The lights shine bright in my eyes. My heart is beating faster than ever. My mouth is dry. I fall into the shadows but the footsteps go on. A shout, a gunshot and I'm gone forever. With only memories left behind.

HARRIET UPTON (10)

Horringer Court Middle School

CHEESE AT 10.32 ON A SATURDAY MORNING

The fridge opened quickly. A hand clawed past all the
food in seconds, grabbing one thing. Cheese. The
monster took the cheese, cut it up, ready with the
toast.
Munch, munch, lovely, yummy, cheese on toast.
The cheese was gone forever, never to be seen
again.

MATTHEW TURNER (10)
Horringer Court Middle School

THE NEXT DOOR NEIGHBOUR

Nervously, Amy crept towards the door. It was an enormous oak door. The brass handles ready to be opened, cautiously, Amy walked inside. Inside the door was darkness. Hearing footsteps, something was coming towards her.

'Hello!' Amy whispered, turning on the light. It was Mr Filch, the next door neighbour.

LIAM KINGHAM (10)

Horringer Court Middle School

INDY DEFEATS A DEMON

'Indy pulls out his best weapon, the abyssal whip,'
shouts the commentator. The demon is released into
the arena.
'Time to kick some butt,' Indy says.
'Oh my God, Indy's charging at the demon, I can't
look,' says the commentator.
'The demon slumps to the ground, Indy's won!'

GUY RODWELL (10)
Horringer Court Middle School

CHRISTMAS MORNING!

I woke up at 5am sharp, longing for the presents I hoped for, stuffed in my sparkling stocking. I ripped off the paper and played with my toys. I crammed some chocolates down my throat and raced to wake my parents. We galloped downstairs for more presents, more magnificent presents.

SIOBHÁN FITZSIMONS (10)

Horringer Court Middle School

REVENGE OF THE SUFFOLK CHICKENS

Tommy went to his chicken hut to collect eggs, they hadn't laid in weeks. Again they hadn't laid.
'You better lay one day or I'll eat you.' That night Tommy fell asleep, chickens everywhere pecking at Tommy ...
Tommy woke up with a pale face, '*Phew!* Just a terrible dream.'

KURTIS BEVAN (11)
Horringer Court Middle School

WINTER'S EVENING!

Vienna was nervously walking through the woods when she heard crunching footsteps scampering closer. Spinning round she saw a small dark shadow with bright red eyes glaring at her. It pounced up onto her, knocking her over. Suddenly it leapt onto her and its fur brushed her cheek.

Miaow!

'Gismo!'

HANNAH GOLDTHORP
Horringer Court Middle School

THE PHANTOM BUNNY OF DEATH

I crept into the large wood. I could just work out the outline of a furry creature in the dark, with eyes that glowed in the black. 'Argh! What do I do? What do I do?' I switched on my torch. It was the phantom bunny of the dead.

WILLIAM HURRELL (10)
Horringer Court Middle School

CHRISTMAS MORNING

Scrambling out of bed, I jumped down the stairs to see if Santa had come to visit me. Immediately, I noticed that under my Christmas tree there were no presents! I turned around slowly and suddenly noticed that there were bundles and bundles of presents on our white marble fireplace!

ALICE CODLING (10)

Horringer Court Middle School

THE MASSIVE BLOB

There's a massive blob rushing through town. I saw it in the mist of the urban streets, it's coming at a terrifying speed, rushing towards me. 'What do I do?'
'No … '
'Looks like a good film,' said Tom.
He stepped outside.
'Argh! Giant blob!' cried someone.
'Oh brother!' smiled Tom.

MAX MORLEY (10)
Horringer Court Middle School

HELLO?

Mary arrived home and found she was alone so she sat in the squishiest armchair and warmed her feet by the fire. Suddenly she heard the door squeak. 'Hello?' No one replied, her heart started thumping. She started sweating. Her black cat jumped on her lap. 'Phew! It was you!'

EMMA TURNER (11)

Horringer Court Middle School

EASTER MORNING

'Whoppee!' screamed Lucy as she jumped sharply out of bed and ran downstairs. Her mum and dad were already perched on the sofa waiting. 'Wow!' screeched Lucy looking at her largest chocolate egg. 'I'm definitely opening that one first.' As Lucy opened it, she heard a bark. 'Cool! A puppy!'

KITTY-MAI MOORE (10)
Horringer Court Middle School

JUMBO JET

There was an intruder hippo, who was going on holiday. It took a long time, so he decided to go to the front of the line and get on the plane. The security guards tried to stop him but he sat on everyone and flew the jet far away.

CHRISTY FITZSIMONS (10)
Horringer Court Middle School

TREASURE

I was playing in the garden when I noticed a strange-looking box. I walked over to the strange box. It was a treasure box! My heart was beating excitedly as I wondered what it might be. I opened it carefully and saw … *crackers*, rats! What really rotten luck!

NICKY JEFFS (10)
Horringer Court Middle School

THE DOG

Happily singing to himself, Bruce stopped and opened his mouth. He'd seen his dog. *His dog!* Why his dog? Why not Harry's cat? The problem was, Harry's cat and Bruce's dog were dead. Bruce stepped back and stared at his dog, his long saluki fur was shining as he ran.

ALEX SLATER (11)
Horringer Court Middle School

ADVENTURES OF SIZZ AND WILLOW - OUR PETS

Sizz, the dog and Willow, the cat, went on an adventure. They visited the zoo. They saw elephants, zebras, monkeys and tigers. Suddenly the tigers escaped and chased the adventurous two up a tree. There they stayed till night fell. They slid down the tree and ran home.

KASSY ENGLISH (9)
Meadow Primary School

THE CURIOUS BIRTHDAY

Kelly was coming home from school. She thought everyone had forgot about her birthday. When she got home, it was dark. She put the light on. Nobody was there. Then people jumped out and shouted, 'Happy Birthday.'
She said, 'You remembered my birthday!'

CAITLIN TAYLOR (8)
Meadow Primary School

A SCARE IN THE TREE HOUSE

Ryan and Anne went up into Ryan's old, brown tree house with his black dog, Timmy. When they got up there, they started eating the chocolate biscuits. Then they heard a rustling in the leaves. Timmy barked. Up popped a head. It was Dad. 'You scared us!' said Ryan.

MARTHA EVANS (8)

Meadow Primary School

THE HOT AIR BALLOON

There was once a hot air balloon. A man called Greentop lived in it. He was travelling the Atlantic Sea when he saw a suffering whale. He hoisted the balloon down and took the whale, examined the whale and made it better. Then he took the whale back home.

NATHAN CATCHPOLE (9)
Meadow Primary School

Molly's Birthday

One freezing night when Molly was sleeping and her mum was in bed, she heard a creaky nose downstairs and found the door opening. But who by? It was her birthday tomorrow and she didn't want her presents to be taken.
It was the people with her lovely presents.

Elizabeth Buckenham (8)
Meadow Primary School

CHRISTMAS

Christmas Eve. I hang my fluffy stocking on the fireplace. Then I walk up the creaky stairs and jump into my bouncy bed. I nearly get to sleep when the creaky stairs make a noise. 'Yes!' I say quietly to myself. 'It's Father Christmas!'
'Hello,' says my mum!

CLAUDIA EARLES (9)
Meadow Primary School

THE DAY AT SCHOOL

One day, a girl called Louise had a horrible day at school. At play time she got pushed into a puddle. She got all her number work wrong and got a detention for the whole week! She had to stay at school all weekend to do her work again.

HOLLIE GOODING (8)
Meadow Primary School

THE LITTLE GOAT

There was once a goat called Maloo. He had escaped from a market and was heading for the woods. In the woods, there was a wolf that liked to eat little goats from the market. Maloo held off the wolf but he knew the end was near. Yummy!

NATHAN CATCHPOLE (9)

Meadow Primary School

HAMSTERBALL

Hamsterball is a ball-shaped hamster. One day Hamsterball went on an adventure to find the legendary food tub. The problem was he couldn't get out of his cage. He looked into his food bowl. It was full of the yummiest food ever.
'Squeak, squeak,' said Hamsterball.

BEN FOWLE (9)

Meadow Primary School

THE BOAT

My mum was driving the boat. I had a dog called Rocky. We were having some sandwiches. Suddenly we crashed. The boat was smoking, we were all scared. We didn't know what to do. Then we phoned the lifeguard and they helped us.

TOM MUTTON (9)

Meadow Primary School

THE END OF THE WORLD

Far, far away, in a galaxy unknown to Man, an alien had a baby that she sent down to Earth. A man saw the baby but it jumped and ate the man's head. Then the baby ate all the heads on the planet.

ALEXANDER GRAHAM (8)
Meadow Primary School

BIONICLE DARK YEAR TIME SLIP

It started in Metrunui. Once a peaceful city, the next a horrible realm ruled by Karzahni. He made a war in the pit against Teridax and was a tyrant ruler of his own realm named after him. The Piraka, the order of Mata Nui and Barraki rebelled and won.

ADAM SAYER (10)

Trimley St Mary CP School

MILLIE THE RUNAWAY DOG

I was out walking with my dogs when Millie, my Jack Russell, got spooked by another dog and decided to run home. She ran out of the park and across two main roads. I found her outside our house, safe and sound.

JACK BECKETT (11)
Trimley St Mary CP School

UNTITLED

In the school break, my family and I went to Cyprus with my sister's friend, Katie. We went bowling, swimming and snorkelling and saw fish by the rocks. We went shopping for souvenirs in Larnaca. On the return flight, my sister spilt tea on her jeans. What a wally!

CHARLOTTE CLARK (10)

Trimley St Mary CP School

THE ADVENTURES OF RUBY RABBIT

Ruby was a quiet rabbit. Well that's what you'd think! When Mazie goes to school, Ruby escapes and meets her friends. Today they were doing a dance competition. When Mazie got home, Ruby had a little Tiara with winner on it. But Mazie never guessed where she had been.

SUMMER VALENTINE (11)
Trimley St Mary CP School

MARVELLOUS MUFFINS

I crouched down below the window and hurled a gigantic stink bomb into the kitchen. Excellent timing as my sister was baking muffins! Suddenly Claire collapsed in a heap and the muffins exploded in a thick green haze. This, I thought, would be a good time to make myself scarce!

CONNOR O'GORMAN (10)
Trimley St Mary CP School

OH NO! I'M A FROG!

'I've had enough of trying to catch the frogs in the morning!' shouted Isabella, the witch.
She went to her purple lair. She decided to make a spell to stop the frogs singing but it went wrong!
They sang even louder because she turned into a frog!

GABRIELLA WALSH (10)
Trimley St Mary CP School

PINKY LOST RABBIT

Pinky was in the hutch when she found a hole. She jumped out and ran and ran. She got lost! Pinky was frightened, she could not find her mum.
Then she heard something, it was her mum. Pinky ran to her and was taken back to the nice, warm hutch.

AMY BARNES (10)
Trimley St Mary CP School

DEATH

I was charging home through the woods, one cold stormy night, when suddenly I was in the air. I could see behind me that I had launched over an enormous tree root. I landed on leaves but it felt hard. I had found the lost dead body of Cyrus.

JACK SMITH (10)
Trimley St Mary CP School

SECRET GIRL

There was a girl called Marie. She was normally shy. She liked to dance in front of television when no one was watching. On the way to school she saw a dance competition poster. It was only after her brother teased her about being too scared to enter, she did!

ZOE UTTING (11)
Trimley St Mary CP School

A MAGIC BALLET DANCER

Susie was in her best lesson, dance. She liked it but she was terrible at it.

'Hello class,' said Mrs Walker. 'Today we will be doing ballet. Our school has been chosen to perform for royalty.'

Susie's spell helped her dance her way into being the best on the night.

ADELE BIGGS (10)
Trimley St Mary CP School

THE COMIC OF JAMIE CUTTER

Agent Jamie Cutter has been called for a mission in Washington, to catch the criminals who robbed the bank. He saw a gang piling money into a car and knew it was them. He got his rope and caught them. Then he got the money and gave it back.

MATTHEW TAYLOR (10)
Trimley St Mary CP School

JACK AND JILL

'Slow down, Jack.'
'Jill, hurry up with that bucket! Argh!' screamed Jack, hitting his head, as he tripped and tumbled down the hill.
Jill ran to save him, 'Argh!' shouted Jill, as she too tumbled right to the bottom.
'Oh great, Jill! You could have brought the water with you!'

OLLIE SMITH (11)
Trimley St Mary CP School

UNTITLED

Fred was a juggler. He entered a competition. For his first trick he juggled balls. For his second trick, he juggled knives. For his third performance, he juggled flaming sticks. He had an accident and burnt his finger badly. He was then unable to participate in the talent show!

RYAN PARKER (10)
Trimley St Mary CP School

THE SURFING TRICK THAT WENT WRONG

Joe was a surfer and showed off about it all the time. One day he entered a competition, he was going to do his best trick. At the competition, all the other surfers were good, so he tried so hard that he crashed and got laughed at by his friends!

LUKE RANNER (10)
Trimley St Mary CP School

LITTLE MISS GYMNAST

Miss Gymnast continually did cartwheels, always knocking people over. Once, Miss Gymnast cartwheeled and knocked Miss Sweetiepie and then Miss Ballerina, making them spill their shopping. It was decided she had to stop! They got Mr Evilpants to pinch her each time she knocked someone. She never did it again.

ELLIE GORDON (10)
Trimley St Mary CP School

SPACE

Smash! A meteor shower crashed into the soft breeze of space. The stars glinted and shone as the emptiness blazed. Anonymously shifting rock, smashing against unknown, fiery fading colours coming to life! The green and blue ball spinning slowly round and around making you dizzy with every stare.

ELLIOT FROST (11)
Trimley St Mary CP School

DEEP BELOW

The massive, dark shape of the whale looms in the ocean like a submarine, moving quickly. The seals scatter as the gigantic whale's 60 tonne bulk tears through the water. They panic, swimming straight into its path. The whale's jaws swing shut on the soft flesh of the seals.

HARRIET HESLOP (10)

Trimley St Mary CP School

DANGEROUS DAD!

One warm, spring day, Dad decided to clean the patio. He mixed some trailer cleaner containing acid with some patio cleaner. He then had a Frank Spencer moment and added bleach to the concoction. Resulting in - a plume of gas similar to the atomic cloud at Hiroshima! *Kaboom!*

EDWARD BLAZA (10)

Trimley St Mary CP School

ANIMAL ESCAPE FROM THE ZOO

It was midnight, Bertie Beaver and Charlie Chipmunk needed their freedom. Bertie banged on the fence, that was their signal. As planned Roger Rhino stampeded into Lizzie Lizard's cage, and she scuttled out. The guards ran after her. Bertie quickly dug a tunnel and whilst nobody was looking, they escaped.

HOLLY TAYLOR (10)

Trimley St Mary CP School

THE MYSTERY IN THE IPSWICH CHANGING ROOM

The Ipswich Town boys had finished training. Jim went to get a cup of tea but it took him over an hour and he had disappeared. Ipswich searched the stadium, they still couldn't find him, they went back to the changing room and found Jim's clothes and an open window.

DANIEL PATTERSON (10)
Trimley St Mary CP School

THE TRIP TO BRIGHTON

One rainy day, a family set off to Brighton for a christening. They left in plenty of time but disaster struck. They got a puncture. The dad changed the tyre but it slowed them down. They made it to the church on time but they were very wet!

JENNA CHURCHMAN (10)

Trimley St Mary CP School

MERMAID MAGIC

There once was a mermaid and she lived under the sea. She had a necklace. Inside the necklace was a pearl but she lost it so her powers faded. She swam to shore as fast as she could, but there was a problem, she didn't have a place to stay.

ELLA PORTER (10)
Trimley St Mary CP School

MYSTERIOUS MANSION SAGA

Miley Cyrus went jogging past a creepy, deserted mansion on the corner of her village. The door flew open with a scary, squeaky creak. Miley entered, it was pitch-black. She fell, bumped her head and fainted.

Later Miley woke up at home screaming - was it a dream?

ABBY FLEMING (10)

Trimley St Mary CP School

THE MONSTER FROM THE ABYSS

The sea was still as Captain Kain steered the Normandy slowly to a stop. Fear surrounded the crew. They let out a terrified gasp as a giant tentacle reached from the sea, wrapping itself around the creaking ship. The Kraken dragged the Normandy under the waves and into the abyss …

CONOR SMITH (11)
Trimley St Mary CP School

UNDERGROUND RICHES

I miss the light, thought one of the miners as he hit the underground rocky wall. *It's hopeless, we're never going to find gold down here*. He hit the wall again aggressively. 'Looks like I spoke too soon!' There was something shiny in the wall. Could it be gold?

ADAM CUNNEW (10)
Trimley St Mary CP School

THE RIDE

Finally, I'm there! I step onboard. As the bar comes down on my lap, I realise it is too late to escape. It is starting, the speed picks up, faster, faster, twisting, twisting. It slows. I feel as if I'm falling, before finally stopping. I've survived the mighty roller coaster.

TOMMY PANE (10)
Trimley St Mary CP School

MY SAGA!

There was once a thirsty man who lived in a caravan, with no water or food. Suddenly, a genie appeared and granted him three wishes. His first was for water, his second was for food and his third was for more wishes. The man was no fool it seemed!

JOSHUA SOAMES (10)

Trimley St Mary CP School

MY HOMEWORK

Today Mrs Smith gave me some homework to write a mini saga. I'm at home now and it's driving me insane to think of interesting subjects and I am limited to only fifty words. At the moment my mind has gone completely blank. Will I get anything done in time?

ELLIE ANTHONY (10)
Trimley St Mary CP School

FOOTBALL ALIENS

Trimley Red Devils were playing a new team. The team kept cheating by jumping into positions. Suddenly the Trimley keeper floated up and the ball went in. The ref looked up and a spaceship came through the clouds. The players and ref melted into green aliens.

JAMIE POLLARD (10)
Trimley St Mary CP School

LILY AND NUGGET

One day, Lily saw a dog without a lead. Worried, she ran up to it fast. Picking up the small dog, she took it to her house. Fortunately her mum let her keep it. Smiling at the dog, she named it Nugget. She and Nugget were friends from then on.

CELINA CHAN (10)
Trimley St Mary CP School

THE LEGEND OF ROBIN HOOD

Once upon a time, in Sherwood Forest, Robin Hood devised a plan. When he saw a man walk by, he jumped out and scared him. Consequently the man fled, terrified. Robin Hood smugly thought, *it's a lot easier now I've decided to rob the poor to give to the rich!*

SEBASTIAN HOW (10)

Trimley St Mary CP School

THE MAGIC MAP

Ben and Lola found a dazzling map. They fell into it, they ended up outside a castle. They knocked on a door and a witch opened it, they said, 'Hi! We came here by magic and we can't get home.'
The witch cast a spell and they returned home.

ADRIANA CREMER (10)
Trimley St Mary CP School

GOLDILOCKS HAS A DAY OUT

One day, Goldilocks was walking and found a house full of lovely chocolate bars and flowers. Goldilocks ate lots of chocolate until she felt sick and took some flowers and went home. Walking home, she felt guilty about taking the flowers without asking for them.

JOSHUA HICKS (10)

Trimley St Mary CP School

THE ALIEN ARRIVAL

There was an alien who had just landed on Earth. He noticed people staring at him. He made a move and somebody giggled. When he got to a market he didn't know what it was. He saw people buying stuff and he bought something. He flew back home at last.

LAUREN BOND (11)
Trimley St Mary CP School

THE BLACK SPIRIT

One night, there was a terrible storm. Melody was riding home on her horse. *Flash!* Lightning struck. The horse panicked and threw Melody to the ground. *Flash!* The horse disappeared. Melody lay frightened and crying on the wet ground. Suddenly a black horse appeared and showed her the way home.

MADELINE PROCTOR (10)
Trimley St Mary CP School

THE DAY MY DOG CAME TO SCHOOL

Today I took my dog to school, he helped me in all my lessons, even maths. After maths we had PE. We played basketball (but he couldn't bring the ball back). Then rounders but he buried the baton! At lunchtime, we had hot dogs of course!

DANIEL KING (11)
Trimley St Mary CP School

ARE WE NEARLY THERE YET?

The three immature children climbed into the back of the family car, eager to start their holiday to Cornwall. Ten minutes into the journey, they started, 'Are we nearly there yet?'
This was repeated every ten minutes as they took it in turns. Eventually they arrived at the hotel.

ROSIE RETALLICK (10)

Trimley St Mary CP School

A DISTURBING BREAKFAST

The princess was eating a gorgeous meal when the Earth trembled. As the dangerous dragon rose from its sleep, the princess grabbed her sword and stabbed it into the dragon's heart. The dragon roared at the distant stars like a wolf howling at the moon, then fell with a thud!

SARAH MCLAREN (11)
Trimley St Mary CP School

MACK AND LILL

Mack and Lill went up the hill to get some wood for the fire. Lill fell down and broke her leg and Mack came tumbling after. She had to be sent to hospital and cried as they had to open her leg up and Sellotape the bone back together.

AMY SIDNEY (8)
Tudor CE (VC) Primary School

THE GINGERBREAD LAMB

There was a little ginger biscuit in the oven, shaped as a lamb. He was being baked for lunch. When he came out, he jumped off the baking tray and ran out of the front door. His owners chased after him. The ginger lamb fell in a river and drowned.

JAI MCCRORY (8)
Tudor CE (VC) Primary School

BUSTER

Yesterday, Buster got out of the kennel and got dressed for work. He got in his car and drove to work. When he got to work, his paper had all gone so he went home. He entered his kennel and made a hot chocolate!

REBECCA MCHUGH (8)

Tudor CE (VC) Primary School

PETER'S BOOK

It all began in the house. Peter was in Mum's room, looking under the bed. He found a book. The book read 'Do not open, bad things will happen to you.' Peter opened the book. The house shook. It was a stampede. He ran to the police for help!

BAILEY ANDREWS (8)
Tudor CE (VC) Primary School

BOB

'Why me?' Bob asked. Bob was swimming along and a shark came swimming by. He had red eyes and teeth like swords. *Snap!* He ate Bob all in one go. A net fell into the water.
'Why me?' said the shark. The fisherman sliced his belly open.
'Thanks!' said Bob.

GEORGINA CHAMLEY (10)
Westley Middle School

WHY ME?

'Why me?' Me and my mum went to Australia for a holiday. My mum went to have a bit of a splash in the sea. A shark came cruising by and gobbled her up in one piece. Now I'm stuck on the other side of the world, on my own.

BETHANY STEVENS (10)
Westley Middle School

THE 9TH KEY TO THE KINGDOM

'Why me?' Ben questioned. He must not die, for he held the ninth key to the kingdom. Erea, the princess, needed that key! Just then a flash of light exploded and Princess Erea stepped out of the light, for she knew that Ben would die. Such determination, such loyalty!

ELLIE FREEMAN (10)
Westley Middle School

THE SUPER DOG

'Why me?' I screamed. I was falling out of a crashing aeroplane at 10,000 feet high. I was frightened and thought it was the end. When I was 50 feet above the ground, Super Dog flew up and grabbed me and took me safely to the ground.

HARRIET DINKELE (10)
Westley Middle School

DANGERS OF CROWDS

He was in the midst of a crowd but stumbled. When he hit the cold gravel, he reached for the hand of his dead mother. He screamed but he had a smug smile on his face! This was as he had planned!

JACK ELLIOTT (10)

Westley Middle School

IT

There 'it' was, lying there, eyes open, screaming 'its' eyes out. You could see how happy Dad was. He picked 'it' up and stared saying, '*Ssshhh!*' We took Mum and 'it' home. Gran was waiting for us, she seemed to have forgotten me. I hated 'it'. Every last part.

LEAH VERMEULEN-COLE (10)
Westley Middle School

A WINDY NIGHT

On a windy night, a boat rocked side to side with the pirates going 'Ho, ho!' The sun was gazing on them. A submarine was looking up, then suddenly a torpedo shot and hit the ship on the stern. The ship rocked, silently dropping to the bottom of the sea.

EDWARD SPURLING (10)

Westley Middle School

THE GHOSTS

She stood there, staring out the shop window. 'You know when you just stare out at space, you tend to see things like ghosts.'
'Yeah, I suppose, but they're not real.'
'That's what you think, sometimes I have psychic vibes, I see ghosts.'
'Whatever!'
'Seriously, it's true, look behind you!'

ABBIE MOORE (11)
Westley Middle School

LITTLE BOW KEEP AND HER PIGS

The pigs wandered into the field. Little Bow Keep followed. She pulled out her wand, zapped a pig. It turned into an ornament. She put it in her pocket and continued.

The next day the pigs decided to rebel, they found her wand, zapped her, broke it like a twig.

CHARLOTTE ORRISS (10)
Westley Middle School

THE NEVER-ENDING RIDE

He kept falling, wishing he hadn't got on the roller coaster. He never liked roller coasters and now wished he'd held on. He kept falling until finally he stopped, his heart racing. He opened his eyes to see nothing but darkness, he'd fallen into nothingness, never to be seen again.

LILY MAGUIRE (10)

Westley Middle School

LOCH NESS MONSTER

He was in the car and he looked out the window.
'Mum, Mum, look it's the Loch Ness monster.'
Mum stopped the car. She shouted, 'Get the camera!'
She took the camera, she took the picture. Then the
monster ate the camera, then us.
'They taste like warm roast!'

GARETH BORRETT (11)
Westley Middle School

FANCY DRESS PARTY

As David sat up the tree, he saw the cars looking like ants. The toddlers on tricycles going round as if whirling down a plughole. 'David, come down from that tree.'

'You're still going to the party,' smiled Mum.

'Yes, but I'm not going as a fluffy bunny!' he shouted.

EMILY WILLIAMS (11)
Westley Middle School

THE BIG GAME

It was up to the last four. They were playing against the best eight players in the country. The other four had hurt themselves. Ben took the ball but then the other team took the ball. It was ten seconds till the end. Joe smacked it. 'Goal!' They had won.

AMELIA THOMPSON (10)
Westley Middle School

WHAT'S IN THE MIST?

The man crawled out of the bush covered in cuts and bruises. The mist came rolling in, the lights flickered. Closer and closer, he came then . . . *bang!* It hit him. With a scream and a cry, it was over. His life was gone with no warning. Just gone, gone forever!

CARLA BUGG (11)
Westley Middle School

THAT GIRL

Jake was scared. He wasn't just scared, he was petrified. The next day he nearly fainted. It was that girl, that girl with golden hair, glittering silver blood and icicles for fingers. She was out to get him with her gang, and solid gold knife. Suddenly, *stab*, Jake was dead!

SUZANNA SPENCER (10)

Westley Middle School

THE SCARY NIGHT

It is dark! 12pm to be precise. Daniel is woken up by a noise. *Creak! Creak!* Daniel pulls his cover over his head. He hears footsteps; they are getting closer. Daniel pulls his cover down to have one last look. The door gently swings open with a scary noise. *Eeerrr!*

DANIEL DAVIS (11)
Westley Middle School

SNOW IN SUMMER

I woke up and looked outside to find five inches of snow. I woke my dad up. He looked outside and couldn't believe it because it was in the middle of summer! We went out in our hats. Before we could even pick up a snowball, the snow had melted.

HARRY PAGE (10)
Westley Middle School

IT DISAPPEARED!

I was boiling hot and in the lonely desert. I reached for my very last few drops of water but the bottle had disappeared.

ROSIE HUDSON (10)
Westley Middle School

BEING COOKED

I am the sun's meal in summer's death trap, boiling as
I speak but as I reach out to a small pond, all water
just disappears.
Am I dreaming? Then my eyes creak open and
there's my room! So I am dreaming. Well now,
everything's back to normal.

GEMMA KITCHIN (10)
Westley Middle School

THE HIMALAYAN MYTH

I am climbing one of the Himalayan mountains,
Mount Everest, to prove the myth of the Yeti.
Outside the Yeti cave, I hear thumping and crunching,
heart pounding. I take a picture then run for my life,
dropping the camera. Too scared to stop. Still no
proof of the Yeti!

CHRISTOPHER ARBON (10)
Westley Middle School

THE MISCHIEVOUS PIG!

That pig! It's escaped again, what am I going to do?
Mum will kill me. I tried to bribe Curly back with
some slops. So I set off with the food. Unfortunately,
some dogs chased me and now I've ended up here,
in casualty, in serious pain.

EMMA WARFORD (11)
Westley Middle School

SUPER BANANA

That thing, I think it's called a banana. But it's not a normal banana, it's Super Banana.
Super Banana picked up his banana phone and the chief banana said, 'A banana robber is robbing shops.'
'I will be there right away!' Super Banana caught the robber!

ETHAN YOUNG (10)
Westley Middle School

THE LOST LEGION OF WORLD WAR I

It's the legend of the Lost Legion of World War I.
The legend goes that the commander still gallops the poppy fields every 11th of November.
Thud, thud. The commander gallops past with his gun held to the heavens, poppies bleeding from his heart.
He will return next year.

WILLIAM BOWER (11)
Westley Middle School

MIRACLE

It was leaking tears in the pond where sorrow dripped. It reached for life. It drowned an excruciating death. Its faith gave it a luminous light of hope. Its spirit rose up into a final place; a gloomy but unique place where it struggles to remember …

ADELLE WOOD (10)
Westley Middle School

THE MYSTERY!

'Why me?' I don't understand what happened. I was walking home from school and suddenly someone pulled me in the car. I was terrified. They took me up to the house. They put a gun to my head and *bang!* I was gone!

ELEANOR CATCHPOLE (10)
Westley Middle School

THE DRAGON

The ghastly dragon was breathing heavily in his deep sleep within his gloomy lair. As he awoke he lunged towards his beloved treasure and discovered it had vanished. The dragon's heart throbbed in agonised fury and he roared like thunder. They had stolen the treasure. He would have his revenge!

MEGAN WARNOCK (10)
Westley Middle School

THE AFTER SCHOOL ADVENTURE

As I was walking home from school, I heard a loud wail. It came from a creepy old house. I crept through the open door and sidled up the hall. My heart missed a beat. I screamed. Blood trickled down the hall mirror. Then I heard the laughter. 'April fool!'

OLIVIA CHADWICK (11)

Westley Middle School

JOURNEY TO SCHOOL

As I walked through the woods to school, the footsteps got closer. I was terrified. I ran but they were right behind me. The light appeared through the trees. I was nearly there. Suddenly a tap on my shoulder, I turned to see … my sister! I'd forgotten my lunch box!

MOLLY ROBSON (10)
Westley Middle School

INFORMATION

We hope you have enjoyed reading this book - and that you will continue to enjoy it in the coming years.

If you like reading and writing, drop us a line or give us a call and we'll send you a free information pack. Alternatively visit our website at www.youngwriters.co.uk

Write to:
Young Writers Information,
Remus House,
Coltsfoot Drive,
Peterborough,
PE2 9JX

Tel: (01733) 890066
Email: youngwriters@forwardpress.co.uk